Sinéad
Butler

The Roo
THAT WON THE
MELBOURNE CUP

JACKIE FRENCH

The Roo THAT WON THE MELBOURNE CUP

JACKIE FRENCH

Illustrated by Carol McLean-Carr

An imprint of HarperCollins*Publishers*

AN ANGUS & ROBERTSON BOOK
An imprint of HarperCollinsPublishers

First published in Australia in 1991 by
CollinsAngus&Robertson Publishers Pty Limited (ACN 009 913 517)
A division of HarperCollinsPublishers (Australia) Pty Limited
4 Eden Park, 31 Waterloo Road, North Ryde, NSW 2113,
Australia

William Collins Publishers Ltd
31 View Road, Glenfield, Auckland 10, New Zealand

HarperCollinsPublishers Limited
77-85 Fulham Palace Road, London W6 8JB, United Kingdom

National Library of Australia
Cataloguing-in-Publication data:

French, Jacqueline.
    The roo that won the Melbourne Cup.

    ISBN 0 207 16779 6 (HB)
    ISBN 0 207 17329 X (PB)

    Kangaroos — Juvenile fiction. I. Title

A 823.3

Typeset by Excel Imaging Pty Ltd, Sydney
Printed in Hong Kong

5 4 3 2 1
95 94 93 92 91

*For my mother, who tackles life like Aunty Mug,
for Fred the wallaby, and for Edward with love*

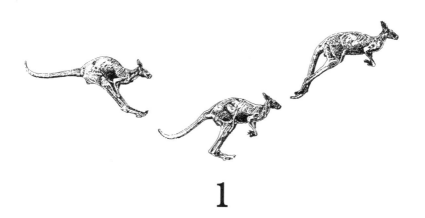

1

'*. . . and they're coming round the home turn now and it's Rosie's Child in the lead, Blue Bottle second, No Regrets and Captain's Nancy, Jerilderie, Sultan's Choice, Play my Fancy and Southern Cross followed by Aunty Flo on the outside . . .*'

Annabelle and Bernie opened the door quietly. The kitchen smelt of wood from the stove, old teapots and wet fur from the hessian sack suspended from a chair. Aunty Mug sat in a chair by the wireless, her gumboots in the oven. She looked up at them, nodded, and put her finger to her lips. They closed the door and sat down and waited. Annabelle looked out the window, at the overgrown garden and the paddocks and hills beyond. Bernie poked down into the hessian sack. A small hairy face peered out, and sucked his finger for a second. He picked the animal out. It was a wombat, still with the

1

soft fur of a baby. Annabelle leant over to stroke it too.

'. . . *and they're coming around the turn into the straight . . .*' announced the wireless over a burst of static. '. . . *Rosie's Child is out in front, No Regrets's coming from the inside, Blue Bottle and Captain's Nancy, Aunty Flo two lengths behind, Blue Bottle, Homeward Bound, Great Expectations leading Honour Bright with Red Rascal at the rear, it's Rosie's Child leading by two lengths to No Regrets, she's pulling away, it's Rosie's Child, Captain's Nancy, Aunty Flo making ground on the outside now, Captain's Nancy and Jerilderie are neck and neck, followed by Sultan's Choice, Play my Fancy, Southern Cross, but it's Rosie's Child, Rosie's Child all the way, Rosie's Child goes on to win . . .*'

'Goes on to win! Goes on to win!' cackled a voice from the windowsill. A white cockatoo flapped its wings, then settled back in its cage again. It stropped its beak against the bars of the cage.

Another crackle of static burst from the wireless and Cliff Carey's voice edged into an advertisement: '*Rich Red Fountain Tomato Sauce . . .*' Aunty Mug turned him down and lifted her gumboots out of the oven and onto the cracked lino floor.

'It's not like being there,' she sighed, wriggling her toes into them again. 'No smell of horses and silk and hot grass, and bell-toppers bobbing by the enclosure. There's nothing like a real horse race. You don't put on a black velvet hat and a spot of lipstick to listen to the wireless. But it's better than nothing.'

'Dad says we'll all have television in a few years,' said Bernie as he scratched the wombat behind the ears. 'Then you'll be able to see it. You'll be able to see the whole race. It'll be just like the movies in your own house.'

Aunty Mug shook her head. 'It still won't be like being there. You don't get the smell of it all at the movies. Horses smell different on the course — oats and brushing and spit and polish. You can smell the women's perfume and the men's tweed. It's all very well for your father to talk. I'll believe in this television when I see it.'

'I've seen it,' said Annabelle. 'It was in a shop window when I was down in Melbourne with Angie and her mother. There was a crowd around it, but Angie and I wriggled down to the front. We had afternoon tea, too, in a real cafeteria. Pikelets and cream and a raspberry milkshake.'

'Oh, I know television exists,' said Aunty Mug. 'But you can't tell me the day will ever

4

come when people like me or your father can afford it.'

She leaned back in the chair. 'Well then,' she demanded. 'How was your week?'

Bernie sighed. 'Awful,' he said.

'Terrible,' said Annabelle.

Aunty Mug looked at them in surprise. 'What's the matter?'

'It's Dad,' explained Annabelle. 'He wants me to leave school after the Scholarship next year and get a job in the bank. Says it's a good standby for a girl.'

'And he wants me to leave and take up an apprenticeship with him,' put in Bernie.

Aunty Mug raised an eyebrow. 'Well, what's wrong with that?'

'Everything,' said Annabelle. 'Who wants to leave after the Scholarship? I'll only be just turned thirteen.'

'Lots of other kids leave that young,' said Aunty Mug. 'I did. Your dad did. We've done all right.'

'It's not just that,' explained Annabelle. 'I couldn't stand being stuck in an office all day.'

'Any other ideas?' asked Aunty Mug.

Annabelle looked at her hands, then looked up. 'I want to work with animals. I want to be a vet,' she said. 'But it'd cost an awful lot of money. It'd mean getting the bus to Burrengong every day to the high school, then going down to Melbourne to the university.'

'Your father should be making enough,' said Aunty Mug. 'What's wrong with the idea?'

'Girls can't be vets,' said Bernie.

Aunty Mug looked at him sternly. 'You listen to me, my lad. I was a girl once and there was nothing I couldn't do. This is the 1950s, not the 1890s.'

'You're different,' said Bernie.

'Maybe Annabelle is too,' said Aunty Mug. 'You mark my words. One day the time will come when there are just as many women vets as men. Anyway, what's wrong with you doing an apprenticeship? I thought you liked engines.'

'Not all day, Aunty Mug. You know what I want to do. I want to go to agricultural college, then work here with you.'

Aunty Mug looked at them both. 'Well, what did your father say when you told him about these schemes of yours?'

Annabelle looked at Bernie, looked back at Aunty Mug. 'We didn't tell him,' she admitted.

'Great fish and little apples! May I ask why not?'

Bernie shrugged. 'You know Dad when he's angry,' he said.

'He's so touchy since Mum died,' said Annabelle.

'He's got every right to be touchy,' said Aunty Mug. 'He's got his work to do and you two to bring up by himself. But I know my younger brother. You tell him straight out what you want and see how he takes it. You're a pair of drongos, the both of you.'

Bernie glanced at Annabelle. 'We were hoping you might speak to him,' he suggested.

Aunty Mug snorted. 'You fight your own battles,' she said. 'If someone else does your fighting for you, the victory's not worth much. If you want something enough, you need to work for it. If you care enough, you'll get it. If you lose the first time, you just try again.'

Annabelle sighed. 'We were afraid you'd say that,' she said.

'I've said it often enough about a lot of things,' said Aunty Mug. 'It's true.' She stood up.

'It was a good race,' she said. 'Come on. Let's go outside. I want to feed Blossom, and we'll have a look at the horses on the way. Put Harold back in his sack. It's too cold for him outside.'

'Does he need a feed?' asked Bernie.

Aunty Mug shook her head. 'I just gave him

THE ROO THAT WON THE MELBOURNE CUP

one before you came in,' she said. 'Let him
sleep. You can give him his next feed later.'

Aunty Mug had had Harold for two months.
He was hairless when the trappers brought him
in after they had caught his mother. Aunty Mug
still fed him every three hours, even through the
night, with a bottle and a special teat she'd
made from the rubber end of an eye dropper —
milk and egg yolk and cod liver oil and some
charcoal from the fire. Babies were easier than
wombats, said Aunty Mug, who'd never had a
baby.

Aunty Mug liked animals. As well as
Harold, there were Herb and Blossom, the goats
in the orchard.

'Goat's milk suits me,' said Aunty Mug. 'A
bottle full of squirting and you're done. We'd
never get through a bucketful from a cow, me
and the animals.'

There was Pig Iron Bob, the cockatoo in his
cage on the kitchen windowsill. The cage was
never shut, but Pig Iron Bob felt safe there, and
only left it for a hop around the verandah in the
mornings. Aunty Mug had found him caught in
a fence with one leg mangled and a broken wing,
and he'd stayed with her ever since. Pig Iron
Bob had a yellow crest that was always mussed
up from hopping under the verandah chairs. Just

like a single hairy eyebrow, said Aunty Mug.

There was Jeremiah the gander, who lead his team of geese through the fruit trees. Aunty Mug had bought him and his mate, Lamentations, to breed and then to eat, but she could never bring herself to kill them. Every year they raised more goslings, and the goslings grew and raised more too. There were thirty geese under the apple and plum trees now.

There was Bert, too, another wombat. He was four years old, but still wandered in at night when he was feeling friendly. He liked the warmth of the stove and the warm bread and milk Aunty Mug put out for him. Bert snored, said Aunty Mug, but he was good company. Bert was the reason Aunty Mug had put a screen door on the kitchen, that you could push either way. Otherwise, Bert would push through the wall.

Then there was Fred. Fred was kangaroo-in-residence. He was too big now to live inside, except for visits at meal times. But he still hung around the house.

Aunty Mug liked to have a kangaroo around the house. 'The trouble with humans is they're all the same. It's good to get to know another species. But there aren't too many you can share a house with. If you get a cat, you end up waiting on them, breakfast in bed and service when they want you to open the door. Goats smell, you can't toilet train a horse. But a roo'll do its business outside, after it's eaten — and it'll get most of its food for itself after a while. All a roo wants from you is your friendship and a bit of warmth by the fire and a snack or two. And to see a mob of roos dance across the hills at sun-up — that's the most beautiful thing in the world.'

Everyone knew Aunty Mug. If an animal was injured on the road, or if someone shot its mother, it was a safe bet to bring it to Maureen Halloran. She'd look after it. If anyone could rear an orphaned animal, it was Aunty Mug.

There were no dogs. Aunty Mug loved dogs. But you can't have dogs and kangaroos, said Aunty Mug, or dogs with wombats or lame cockatoos. Dogs are hunters, and other animals know it. You've got to choose.

Once there had been horses, too, at Redgate Farm. That had been in the days when the children's grandfather was alive, and a few years after, when Redgate trained runners for every big race in the country. Aunty Mug had run the farm with her father, then by herself as he got too old. Aunty Mug was fifteen years older than her brother, the children's father. He'd taken his apprenticeship, but Aunty Mug had no time for machines. She stayed with the farm and her animals.

Aunty Mug loved horses too much to be a successful trainer. She was too attached to them. Any horses, from old Sampson who was nearly thirty now and who'd pulled a plough before the war, to Golden Queen who'd won the Geelong Cup twenty years ago and still grazed the lower paddock. There were other horses too, winners from old races and ones who'd never won at all. Aunty Mug had bred them all, and loved them.

'Where's Fred?' asked Bernie, looking round.

Aunty Mug put her fingers in her mouth and whistled. The noise echoed round the courtyard and sheds and yards. There was a thumping behind the shed and Fred bounded out. He was taller than Aunty Mug now, and almost twice as wide, a giant of an eastern grey. His back was dusty where he'd been lying in the sun. He came up behind Aunty Mug and put his furry arms around her neck.

'Aaaagh,' he said as he held his head down to be scratched.

'Get off,' said Aunty Mug. 'Come on, you great galoot. You tickle. Come round in front.'

Like Harold, Fred had come to Redgate

Farm as an almost hairless baby after shooters got his mother. He was fully grown now, but still loped around the farm, sampling horse tucker and jumping at the geese.

'I bet he's the biggest roo around,' said Annabelle proudly as she scratched his ears.

'He eats enough,' said Aunty Mug. 'No-one'd believe now how tiny he was when those shooters brought him in. I never thought I'd raise him, not all bald as a rat like he was. No, get your big nose out of my pocket, Fred. There's no tucker for you there. You're old enough to get your own food.'

'Could I get him some bread? Please Aunty Mug?'

'There's some stale in the top of the bread bin,' said Aunty Mug. 'You're spoilt, Fred. That's your trouble.'

'Aaaagh,' said Fred. He leant back on his tail and lifted one great foot playfully. Aunty Mug pushed it back down. 'None of that,' she said. 'You're too big, Fred. You can hurt someone like that.' She shook her head. 'You've got to be careful with boy roos. I had one rip up a dog of mine once. That was the last dog I ever had. The roo was Roger. He was big, but not as big as Fred. I said then I'd never have another boy roo, they get too stroppy, I'd stick to the girls. But I couldn't refuse Fred when they brought him in. No bigger than a skinned rabbit, were you Fred, and eyes like a baby possum's.'

Annabelle and Bernie had watched Fred grow up. Their home was in the town, three miles away. But since Mum died and with more and more cars in town, Dad spent more and more time in the workshop. It was an easy bike ride to Redgate Farm, and more fun than the smell of petrol.

'How's your father?'

'Busy,' said Bernie. 'He's got Johnny Wilkins working on the petrol bowser now in the mornings. It gives him more time in the workshop. There was some bloke from Melbourne up to see him during the week. Something about putting in a showroom to sell cars too.'

Aunty Mug snorted. 'There are enough cars around here as it is without your father trying to sell more. I remember when there were only a dozen cars in the district and if you went to town in one you'd need to pack your lunch in case it broke down. But he's always been like that, your father. Give him an engine and some grease and he'll be happy. He likes his pennies too. Well, he's working for them and I reckon he'll get them.'

'What's wrong with money?' asked Bernie.

'Nothing's wrong with money. Not as long as you still live your life while you're making it.'

Bernie looked at her. 'Would you have liked more money, Aunty Mug?'

'Too right,' said Aunty Mug. 'But you know something? I wouldn't change one bit of my life to get it. I know what they say, that I've wasted my time with strays when I could have been training horses. That I wasted my time with animals like Fred and Bert and Harold. Wasted time! Wombats and kangaroos were here before any horse. I reckon if you love animals you love all of them, not just the ones that make you money or that you eat. I could have a stud with white fences now, like that old Dan Coates down the road at Girrinwilli. But I wouldn't give up one of my friends to have it. Not Fred or Harold or Pig Iron Bob, or any of the animals through the years. Not one.'

Bernie watched her talk. She didn't have much, Aunty Mug. She hadn't had a new car since before the war, never had a holiday, never bought a fridge or a washing machine or a mixmaster or any of the exciting things you could buy nowadays. But she had time. She listened to you. She talked like no-one else ever did. He wondered if it would be possible to be like Aunty Mug but still earn money too.

They walked through the yard together, over the hard, beaten soil, too hard-packed from horses' hooves ever to grow grass again, past the stables, nearly empty now, past the track to the orchard and over to the fence by the paddock. Fred loped at their heels, hoping for a walk.

Aunty Mug leaned over the railings. 'Look at Golden Queen,' she said. 'Shines in the sun, doesn't she? She was like that when I named her. Only two weeks old, and it was raining, and just as I was looking at her the sun came out and a shaft hit her coat. It was pure gold. "You're a Golden Queen," I told her, and she was too. She's a horse and a half. Got a stride like Betty Cuthbert. Did I ever tell you how she won the Geelong Cup? Fifteen to one, and they'd boxed her in at the rails, but young Terry Jeffrey, you don't get jockeys like that any more, he took her to the outside and held her there, with a clear view in front of her all the way. You can't box a horse like Queenie in. Only a horse like Queenie could have made it. She ate the last lap like it was toast and marmalade, and I was crying so much I hardly saw her at the finishing post. Even Dan Coates had to admit I'd done it that time.'

The children listened absently. They'd heard the story before. They'd heard most of

Aunty Mug's horse-racing stories.

'I tried to breed her later, but she didn't take. Why should she? She's like me, not cut out to be a mother. You can't run with the wind in your hair when you're in foal. I bet she remembers it though, the cheering and the yelling and the betting slips showering in the wind like a snow storm by the ring, and that strut around the paddock at the end, when the world is looking at you and you know it.'

'How old is she now?' asked Annabelle absently.

There was no answer. She looked round. 'Aunty Mug! What is it?'

There were tears on Aunty Mug's cheeks. 'You get to remembering,' she explained, fishing in her pocket for a hanky. 'There's nothing wrong with remembering. I remember when there were two dozen horses in the yard. I remember when there were half a dozen lads working here. Then the depression and the war and Dad dying, and your Uncle Ron. I could never build it up again. You realise that that's all you've got, your memories. I bet even Fred'd beat any horse I've got now. I'll never win another race. I'll never walk the ring again, or watch the tote and say, "That number's mine", or feel the world is stopping when they say you've won. Not even a small race. I'm like Queenie. I'm past it now.'

'Not you!' declared Bernie.

'You're not past it!' said Annabelle. 'You can still do anything. I bet you could still win a race if you wanted to. Look at Mr Coates. He must be years older than you, and his stables are getting bigger all the time.'

Aunty Mug smiled through her tears. 'Dan Coates is exactly seven months and three days older than me,' she said. 'We started school the same day together, and I bet him my frog would beat his lizard down the school verandah, but the teacher confiscated both of them before we could have a go. You're right. It's not old age. It's the way I've gone about things. The horses Dan trains now, they're other people's. He expanded. I stayed small. I just wanted a few animals that I loved. And you know something? If I did it all again, I wouldn't change a thing.'

'No regrets, Aunty?'

'None at all.' She grinned. 'Well, one,' she admitted. 'I always wanted a runner in the Melbourne Cup. I'd still give almost anything just for that. I thought Queenie might make it, but she didn't. She went lame two days before the Caulfield. But we almost did, didn't we, old girl?'

As though she heard her name, Queenie looked up. She trotted over and thrust her head at Aunty Mug's shoulder. 'No, there's nothing there,' said Aunty Mug. 'You had your apple this morning. Get out of it, you lazy creature. What you want's a run.'

She handed the bucket to Annabelle. 'Here, mind this,' she said. 'Out of the way, Fred. Do you have to get your nose in everything?' She slipped through the railings. 'Hold still, you great galoot,' she said. 'We're neither of us any younger.' Suddenly she was on her, barebacked, without reins or bridle. She patted Queenie's neck and they were off.

Annabelle and Bernie watched them go.

'She can ride!' said Bernie. 'I'd like to see anyone ride like Aunty Mug.'

'Yeah, like Jimmy Farrel's dad. He thinks he's so smart. I'd like to see him do what Aunty Mug can with a horse.'

The horse and rider were galloping now. Aunty Mug's hair had come unpinned and streamed behind them like Queenie's tail. She leaned into the horse's neck and directed the stride with a gentle touch of her hand.

'Aaagh,' said a voice behind them. It was Fred. He watched the horse and rider for a moment, then suddenly he was through the fence too, leaping across the paddock, bounding towards Aunty Mug. The horse seemed to sense him. She galloped faster. You could almost hear the cheers of the crowd in her ears. Her hooves echoed on the hard ground. Fred gained steadily. He was bounding beside them now, pacing them easily, his giant feet pushing casually at the ground, his tail almost level behind him. Finally, he turned for home. Aunty Mug turned Queenie to follow. Queenie was sweating, her golden sides shining. Fred reached the fence again fifty yards ahead of them and stopped. He licked his paws thoughtfully.

Queenie was panting. So was Aunty Mug.

She slid off Queenie's back and laughed. 'I needed that,' she said. 'As for you, old girl, it'll help get some of that fat off you.'

'Aaaagh,' said Fred, pleased with himself. Aunty Mug grinned. 'You'd beat the lot of them, wouldn't you Fred?' she said. 'You'd win the Cup if they let you.'

Annabelle scratched Fred under the chin. He arched his back, balanced on his tail, to give her a longer stomach to work on. The hair was softer on his stomach, almost fluffy, and much lighter than his back.

'Could a roo really win a race?' she asked.

Aunty Mug shrugged. 'I don't know,' she

said. 'A roo's a stayer. It'll go for miles. You don't lose much energy in a bound like Fred's. As for sprinting, well, a roo like Fred's fast, but only for a short distance — much less than a horse can sprint. He might have a chance in a longer race.'

'Like the Cup,' said Annabelle.

Aunty Mug stood totally still. Her face was blank. She looked down at Fred as though she hadn't seen him before.

'Aunty Mug, what is it?'

Suddenly, she smiled. The smile grew till it covered her face. 'It's impossible,' she said. 'It really is impossible! We could never do it.'

'Do what?' insisted Bernie.

'Run Fred in the Melbourne Cup.'

'You can't run a roo in the Melbourne Cup!' cried Bernie.

'Why not?'

'It's for horses!'

'Where does it say so?' demanded Aunty Mug. 'Where does it say that kangaroos aren't allowed to run?'

The children stared at her. Aunty Mug's smile seemed fixed to her face. 'Well?' she demanded. 'Said I was finished, did they? Said I had kangaroos in my top paddock? I'll show them what a kangaroo can do. I'll show them I can have a runner in the Cup my own way. Can't run a roo in the Cup? I'm going to have a bloody good try.'

It was warm inside the kitchen. The steam from the morning's kettle had floated up to the ceiling and now dripped from the flaking paint. Pig Iron Bob strutted back and forth in his cage, his feathers ruffled. 'They're lining up at the barriers!' he squawked. 'Lining up at the barriers!'

The wireless kept him company on the mantelpiece. *'Radiator leaks in your car? Try Bardsley's Radiator Compound! Bardsley's for your car! And now back to Flemington and weight's right for the fifth . . .'* Aunty Mug raked over the ashes in the stove till they showed a spark, added tinder and put the kettle on. 'There's bread and honey, bread and jam, or there's cold meat and a lettuce if you want to go down and pick it.'

'Aunty Mug, are you serious?' demanded Bernie.

Aunty Mug looked at him calmly. 'I don't know yet,' she said. 'I'll have to think about it. I want to time Fred properly first. There's no point having a starter that won't finish. I want to see what he'll do on a track, too. For all I know, he might just jump into the stands and leap away.'

'No he won't,' said Annabelle firmly. 'Not if there's anything running in front of him. Fred'll chase anything. Won't you, Fred?'

'Aaagh,' said Fred, reaching out a paw to sneak a slice of bread.

'Paws off,' said Aunty Mug. 'You've had your bread for the day, you big galoot. I'll give you some apple later if you're good. We'll have to give you some training, won't we, boy? Make you start on time and run to the finish.'

'You're really serious,' said Bernie. 'Aren't you?'

Aunty Mug scratched Fred's ears dreamily. He butted his head hard against her. 'All my life,' she said, 'I've wanted a runner in the Melbourne Cup. Now people say I'm finished. Like old Dan Coates, suggesting I sell up and take it easy. Get married, they say. Stop working. Go to tennis parties, join the CWA, make sandwiches for the Bushfire Brigade and lamingtons for the school fete. Ha! Last bushfire I was out there with the best of them, swinging my sack. I've never taken it easy in my life, and I won't start now. Well, I reckon I've got one last chance. If I can't run a horse in the Cup, I'll take what I can get. What about you, Fred?'

'Aaaaaagh,' said Fred.

'You see? asked Aunty Mug.

'. . . *Fighting Spirit out of Flashman's Ghost, owned by R. R. Hillyard, trained by Vern Thompson* . . .' muttered the wireless.

'What now?' asked Bernie.

'We time Fred,' said Aunty Mug. 'Straight after lunch.'

It was cold out in the paddock. The new grass shone green above the frost-bitten brown. The spring wind blew from the hills and cut into them. The horses snickered and stamped their feet. Fred leant back on his tail, the fur on his stomach fluffy from the cold.

'Right, you lot,' said Aunty Mug. 'All organised?'

Annabelle nodded. She was on Golden Queen. Bernie rode Sampson, digging his heels into the horse's fat belly. Aunty Mug was bareback on Darkie. 'He doesn't like a saddle yet,' she explained. 'Time enough for that when he's got used to me. No, don't tell me how Jim Farrel trains his horses. I've got my ways and they're good enough for me. A horse should go with you because it wants to, not because it's scared.'

Bernie dug his heels into Sampson's flanks.

'It's not fair,' he said. 'Sampson'll never keep up with you two.'

Aunty Mug raised an eyebrow. 'You listen to me, young man. That's the biggest part of horse training. The biggest part of life, no matter what you do. You should know that. Learning how to lose. It's what you do mostly and you can never learn too early how to do it gracefully. Then you try again. Come on, up to the starting line.'

The track ran across the paddocks. Twenty years before it had been kept grassed and graded. Now it was all dust and potholes from decades of horses' hooves. On the horizon the hills shimmered in the spring light, gold and green and blue.

'Right,' said Aunty Mug. 'When I say "Go!" I start the stopwatch.'

'Do you think he'll try and race us?' asked Annabelle.

'Only one way to find out,' said Aunty Mug. Darkie snorted, tried to caper. Aunty Mug held him in. 'On your marks. Get set. Get your tail in Fred! Go!'

Queenie leapt first, an old performer, Darkie close behind her, tightly held by Aunty Mug, Sampson in the rear. Fred stood and watched them go. 'Aaaagh,' he said, and scratched his stomach. He seemed to listen to the beat of the horses' hooves. His ears moved slowly forward.

'Aaaagh?' he asked. And then he leapt. Slowly at first, as though he thought they might come back, then he got the idea. His nose went forward, his tail back, his massive feet pushed the ground. Fred was off and running.

He reached Sampson first.

'Aunty Mug!' yelled Bernie. 'He's running!' He looked at Fred, half expecting him to turn and try to play. But Fred's eyes were fixed on Queenie, just ahead, and on Darkie in the lead.

'Aaaagh!' yelled Fred as he bounded past old Sampson.

'Aaaagh!' he acknowledged as he passed Annabelle and Queenie.

'Aaaagh!' he called to Aunty Mug as he drew level with Darkie and raced him neck and neck to the finish.

'What a race!' yelled Bernie, sliding off Sampson.

'He did it,' yelled Annabelle. 'He really raced them!'

Aunty Mug nodded. 'He's got the instinct. That's what a winner needs. The instinct to get in front. Don't get too excited,' she warned them. 'There's many a slip between the cup and the lip. What's he going to do with lots of horses, lots of people, all the noise of a race-track? He might get scared. He might just leap off into the crowd.'

'What next, then?' asked Annabelle.

'We train him,' said Aunty Mug. 'Every morning and evening on this racetrack for two weeks. We teach him to get a move on when the gun fires; we teach him to reach the winning post before he stops. At the end of that . . .'

'Yes?' demanded Bernie.

'We take him to the Bradley's Bluff gymkhana,' announced Aunty Mug. 'We enter him in the Novice Stakes.'

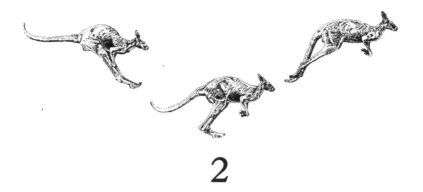

2

The Bradley's Bluff gymkhana was held every year, hosted by the Bradley's Bluff Progress Association (membership fifteen). The CWA sold cakes and cups of tea; the school sold cakes and red or green cordial; the Hospital Committee sold cakes and handicrafts; the Bushfire Brigade Ladies Auxiliary sold cakes and held lucky dips for kids; and the Lion's Club sold beer and steak sandwiches, with a keg of blue ribbon ginger beer for the kids.

Bernie and Annabelle wandered through the crowd. They could smell the burning fat from the Lion's Club tent and dust and horses from the track. The loudspeaker was furry over the creaking record from the merry-go-round. High above them a wedge-tailed eagle circled the clouds as though it knew that today it was safe from humans and their rifles.

'It's a good turn-out,' said Bernie. 'Must be over a hundred people.'

'At least,' said Annabelle. 'Hey, there's Johnny Farrel's dad.'

'Johnny's been skiting all week. He reckons his dad's going to win,' said Bernie. 'He's brought over that big red three-year-old he's been training.'

'Fred'll beat him,' said Annabelle confidently.

'I hope so,' said Bernie. 'I'd love to throw it back at Johnny Farrel that his dad was beaten by a kangaroo. Where is Fred, anyway?'

'Aunty Mug's staying with him in the trailer till just before the race. She doesn't want him scared.'

'Fred's not scared of anything,' said Bernie.

'Aunty Mug knows her business,' said Annabelle. 'She'll get him there.'

'Take your places for the children's obstacle race!' announced the loudspeaker. 'And we have three teams now for the women's tug of war: the Bradley's Bluff Bushfire Brigade Ladies Auxiliary, a new team from the high school and last year's winners, the Fighting Fairies from the pub. We need one more team to make a heat. Come on, all you ladies! Put your names down at the tent.'

30

'Going in it?' asked Bernie.

'Nah,' said Annabelle. 'The pub's got Big Marge. They win it every year.'

A horse snickered from the far end of the field. The crowd moved slowly from the stalls towards the fence. 'I think they're getting ready for the Stakes,' said Annabelle. 'Come on.'

They wandered through the crowd, towards the line of horse boxes that marked the start of the race. A black polo pony cantered out behind the judges' tent and danced its forelegs in the air.

'Hey, Bluey!' yelled Bernie. 'You going to ride that in the Stakes?'

Bluey pulled the pony up. It shook its head nervously and pawed at the ground. He nodded. 'It's Dad's idea,' he answered. 'I was just going in for the tent pegging, but Dad says the race'll quieten him down a bit for the ride home. He was a terror to get here. You riding anything, Bernie?'

Bernie shook his head. 'Not this year.'

'I wanted to enter Golden Queen,' complained Annabelle. 'But they wouldn't let me.'

'Girls can't be jockeys,' snorted Bluey.

'I can ride you into the ground and back again, Bluey Armstrong,' retorted Annabelle.

'That's not the point,' sneered Bluey. 'You might get dirty.'

'You get down here and say that again,' ordered Annabelle, clenching her fists.

'Hey, stop that you two,' said Bernie. 'I want to see what's happening up ahead.'

There was an argument up by the starting post. Bernie and Annabelle pushed forward to hear, leaving Bluey to quieten his pony.

'I still say,' a man was shouting, 'there ought to be a formal barrier!'

'What for?' demanded a thin man in moleskins with a red committee ribbon on his shirt. 'You tell me why, George Fergus!'

'Because it's fairer. That's why.'

There was a laugh behind him. It was Aunty Mug. 'You just want a barrier, George, 'cause your filly took off in the wrong direction last year. You learn to ride and you'll be able to tell her which way to go.'

George Fergus turned. 'You keep out of this, Maureen Halloran.' He stared. 'What's that blooming roo doing here?'

'He's with me,' said Aunty Mug. 'You brought your wife. I brought my kangaroo. Isn't anyone going to start this race round here?'

'You get crazier every year, Maureen

Halloran.' George Fergus turned away, disgruntled.

'Aaaagh,' said Fred as he watched him go. Aunty Mug nodded.

'You're right, Fred,' she said. 'He's like a toad puffed up with hot air. No, you stay here, old boy,' as Fred tried to bound over to investigate another horse float. 'Here, have some bread.' Fred sniffed the slice she handed him, took it carefully and began to nibble. He watched the crowd with interest.

A wiry man in a tweed sports coat strolled over from the judges' tent. It was Dan Coates. He was the same height as Aunty Mug, with the same eyes screwed up from watching horses run in the distance. He looked at Fred suspiciously. 'Are you planning any funny business, Maureen?'

'Good afternoon, Dan,' said Aunty Mug innocently. 'Do you mean me? When have I ever planned any funny business?'

Dan Coates pushed his hat back. 'Who put the tadpoles and the lime jelly crystals in the water jug at the council meeting?' he inquired.

Aunty Mug looked even more innocent. 'Don't ask me, Dan Coates. But they approved the new water treatment plant after that, didn't

they? You don't always have to go the straight way round to get things done.'

Dan Coates snorted. 'You've never done a conventional thing in your life,' he muttered.

'Why thank you, Dan,' said Aunty Mug. 'I reckon that's the nicest thing you've said to me since you took me dancing New Year's Eve and said I smelt nearly as good as a roast dinner.'

Dan Coates looked at her closely. 'What are you planing now, Maureen? Don't tell me you're riding Darkie this afternoon.'

Aunty Mug shook her head. 'He's not ready. Maybe next year.'

'Maybe never,' said Dan Coates. 'He's a wild one. Not even you can train him, Maureen, and it's time you gave up trying.'

'I'll have you know I've had that horse out every morning these past two weeks. He's been a perfect gentleman. You just need to know how to handle him. I plan to have a saddle on him next week. I can train anything,' said Aunty Mug.

Dan Coates snorted. Aunty Mug grinned. 'One day you'll admit it,' she said. 'I bet you anything.'

The horses were lining up now. Old Dusty Morgan was on the far right, pushing ninety, on Belle of the Evening, the oldest 'novice' in the race, so old she had grey whiskers and a stomach like a barrel of beer. Jim Farrel pranced on a fresh red gelding, Bluey Armstrong coaxed his pony, patting her side to calm her down, and a dozen other horses, of varied shapes and sizes, with riders as varied, whinnied and snickered and pushed at the dust with their hooves. High above them a flock of cockatoos cawed, deep white against the blue, waiting for the crowds to go so they could eat the corn and oats from the droppings of the horses.

Annabelle sidled up to Aunty Mug. 'Everything all right?' she whispered.

Aunty Mug nodded. 'I've had him training all week,' she said. 'He's even better than when you saw him last Sunday. He's learnt when a race starts and that you get a bit of apple where it finishes. No late starts today. He'll run like a bat out of hell as soon as the starter fires. You just watch him go.'

'On your marks,' yelled the man with the red ribbon. 'Go when I fire the pistol ... George Fergus, if you don't get that horse lined up it'll be heading for Darwin, same as the one you had last year. On your marks ...'

Bang! The horses' hooves dug into the hard ground. Farrel's red leapt to the front, George Fergus's filly galloped wildly just behind, and a crush of ponies, horses, arms and legs pushed behind them. The crowd cheered along the fenceline, kids with lips red from cordial and lollies, women with strollers and wide skirts, and men with hats pushed back to wipe the sweat and dust from their foreheads, their faces flushed from Lion's Club beer.

'Look at Fred!' yelled Annabelle.

Fred had beaten them all. He'd leapt at the first flash of the gun. Now he was bounding down the track, leading the others by a tail.

'Good old Fred!' screamed Annabelle.

'Look at him go!' shrieked Bernie.

Dan Coates looked at Aunty Mug sternly. 'You and your animals!' he declared. 'That kangaroo of yours could put the horses off their stride.'

Aunty Mug grinned. 'Wouldn't that be just too bad?' she said.

There was a commotion up ahead. The bunch of horses spread suddenly, leaving a dancing pony in their wake.

'Someone's off!'

'Who is it?'

'Bluey Armstrong! Not hurt. He's getting up again.'

'It would be,' said Annabelle, satisfied. 'Now, if I'd been riding . . .' She craned her neck to look at the finish. 'Aunty Mug, I can't see the finish line, how's he going . . .'

It was hard to see the end of the race for dust. The yells had drowned out the music of the merry-go-round and the clink of glasses from the Lion's Club tent.

'Who won?' called someone.

'Can't tell!' came the cry from further up. 'Farrel's red, I think. It's hard to say. That blooming roo ran right through the ribbon and carried it off with him.'

Annabelle giggled.

Aunty Mug winked. 'He's a goer,' she told them. 'He's got the instinct to win. Not that he had much competition today. But it's four times the distance at the Cup. The horses'll be tired while he's still fresh. He'll have a better chance than ever. We're halfway there.'

'Halfway where?' asked Dan Coates suspiciously, overhearing.

'None of your beeswax, Daniel Coates,' said Aunty Mug. 'Let's go up the track and collar Fred before someone grabs him.'

'Where's Bluey? said Annabelle, shielding her eyes. 'I want to rub it in.'

'He's all right. He's over at the drink stand,' said Bernie. 'Hey, Fred's coming back.'

'Aaaagh,' said Fred, loping towards them.

The red ribbon fluttered around his shoulders in the wind.

'Come here, you silly animal,' ordered Aunty Mug. 'Let's take that ribbon off you. Here, I've got a lovely piece of apple just for you. Just what you always get when you cross the finish line.'

'Tent pegging's next,' said Annabelle, scratching Fred's neck. 'Do you want to stay and watch?'

Bernie looked at Aunty Mug. She shook her head. 'Let's get home,' she said. 'We've got some planning to do. We've got a winner to get to the Cup.'

'Aaaagh,' agreed Fred, munching on his apple.

The kitchen table was cleared. Pig Iron Bob was in his cage, spitting apple peel onto the table. Harold's sack hung out of the way by the stove. This was a council of war.

Aunty Mug's hair stuck out at the front from pushing her hands through it. She did it now for the seventh time. 'The more you look at it,' she said, 'the harder it gets. I can't for the life of me see how we can get him entered.'

'It seemed so easy a fortnight ago. There must be some way!' protested Annabelle.

Aunty Mug shook her head. 'A fortnight ago I hadn't thought it through,' she said. 'All I thought of was whether he could win. I still think he'd win if we could get him in the blinking race. But you don't send an unknown horse to the Melbourne Cup. They have to have won before. Stick Fred in the Caulfield Cup or any of the others and he'd be disqualified before we even had a sniff at Flemington.'

'He won today,' put in Bernie.

'I don't think the Bradley's Bluff Stakes counts with the Melbourne Cup committee,' said Aunty Mug. 'You don't put any old backblocks hero in the Melbourne Cup.'

'Maybe he could take the place of another winner,' suggested Bernie.

'If I had another winner who'd get into the Cup, I wouldn't need Fred. Besides, even if we entered him he'd need a jockey. Who's going to ride a kangaroo?'

'Me,' suggested Annabelle.

'You can't,' stated Bernie. 'They don't let women be jockeys.'

'They don't let boys, either,' said Aunty Mug. 'You wait a few years. You need an apprenticeship before you can be a jockey. And I don't see either of you riding Fred. You couldn't. I don't suppose he could carry you, either.'

'There must be some loophole,' said Annabelle.

Aunty Mug sighed. 'You're right. There has to be. I've never been beat before, and I'm not going to be now. Give me a bit of time and I'll find it.'

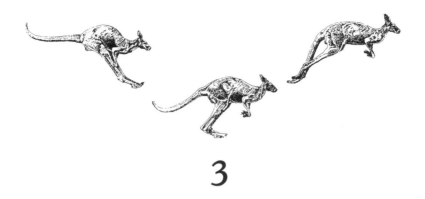

3

'Hey, kids! Customer!'

Bernie looked up from his Phantom comic. It was Councillor Flagon's new Austin. 'I'll get it, Dad!' he called to the oil-stained legs under the hoist. 'Your turn next time,' he said to Annabelle. She was still on her maths homework. She nodded without looking up.

Councillor Flagon strolled around the car and admired its chrome work. 'Your father tells me you'll be working here full-time soon,' he said to Bernie. 'I bet you'll be glad to see the last of school. There's a world of opportunity in the automobile business.'

Bernie smiled grimly as he pumped the petrol up into the bowser. 'That'll be two shillings and seven pence,' he said to Councillor Flagon. Councillor Flagon shook his head and fished the coins out of his pocket. 'Two shillings, sixpence, two halfpennies. That's the only problem with these machines,' he said. 'They cost the earth to run. See you next week, Bernie.'

'Good afternoon, Councillor Flagon,' said Bernie politely. 'And I hope all your tyres burst at once,' he muttered under his breath. He wandered back to the office.

Annabelle looked up. 'What's wrong?' she asked.

'Old Flagon saying how good it'll be when I work here,' he said. 'Dad must have been talking to people.'

Annabelle sighed. The subject of Bernie's apprenticeship and her bank job hadn't been mentioned for a fortnight.

'I think Dad just thinks we'll do what he wants,' she said. 'Maybe we should do what Aunty Mug said. Just come out and tell him we refuse. That we want to go on studying, no matter what he says.'

'You know Dad when he's angry,' said Bernie. 'You tell him.'

Annabelle shook her head. 'I wish Aunty Mug would speak to him,' she said. 'I bet she could find a way round him.'

'She's busy with Fred.'

'I wonder if she's found a loophole yet,' said Bernie as they watched old Mrs Jessup's FB

Holden pass the turn-off by the garage, her green gloved hand waving wildly as she signalled to the non-existent traffic that she was coming out.

'We could ring her up,' suggested Annabelle.

'Nah,' said Bernie. 'She'd never tell us something like that on the phone. Jean or Helen on the exchange'd hear it, and the whole town'd know.'

The Barkers' ute went by, Mr and Mrs Barker in the front, the kids and dogs and bales of hay in the back. Riley's old Vauxhall puttered by, the Harmans' battered Rolls, with its greasy step from lifting sheep in the paddocks, Sam Sergeant's Morris. Annabelle sighed.

The week had stretched endlessly. There was never time to cycle out to Redgate Farm and see Aunty Mug. After school they worked the bowser while their father and his offsider worked under the hoist in the big machinery shed, finishing in time to listen to the Argonauts on the wireless and shell the peas for dinner, to eat the chops or sausages Dad grilled at six o'clock, then do their homework while he went back to the workshop or went out on a call.

Annabelle took up her maths book again and began to study. Bernie gazed out the window. The spring wind blew the big gums along the road and sent the old winter bark scattering down the footpath. The glass top of the bowser glinted in the sun. Next door's kelpie sniffed along the edge of the workshop where oil spread like a black tide, then crossed the tarmac and lifted its leg on the footpath instead.

'You know,' he said, 'I've been thinking.'

'Mmm?' said Annabelle.

'About what Aunty Mug has done for us. You know, when Mum was sick, and she came in every day and cooked and cleaned till Dad got Mrs Hester to come in. She must have had no time for the farm at all. If you want to talk or ask her about things, she's always there. It's time someone did something for her.'

'Like what?' asked Annabelle. 'You heard her. There's only one thing she wants. That's a winner in the Melbourne Cup.'

Bernie was still staring out the window. 'Then she's going to have it,' he announced. 'No matter what we have to do, she's going to have it. Oh no, another customer. I want to finish my comic.'

Half the district came to town on Saturday mornings, and all of them wanted petrol. The men lounged in the driver's side and leaned out the window, got out and watched the meter, or circled their vehicle and kicked the tyres, or wandered over to the workshop while the tank was filling to have a yarn. The women sat in the passenger's side and adjusted their hats to keep out the sun or fixed their lipstick in the mirror. The kids giggled with the dogs and groceries in the back. At half-past eleven, Annabelle went down to the shops to get the groceries: corned meat for lunch, fresh tomatoes and canned beetroot, a high white loaf with a black crust from the baker's and a Neapolitan cake for afters, with thick pastry at the bottom and cream oozing out from between the layers of cake. She made the sandwiches while Bernie served the last of the customers, then put the 'Closed for Lunch' sign out the front. Through the window the washing flapped on the clothes-line, held up with wattle props. Next door's cat wandered round the geranium bushes, then squatted on the thin lawn. Even here in the kitchen, the house smelt of oil — Dad's overalls in the washing basket for Mrs Hester to pick up on Monday, his boots on the doormat.

Bernie came through from the front, wiping his hands.

'Give Dad a yell,' said Annabelle. 'The kettle's on.'

'Dad!' yelled Bernie out the door.

'Coming!'

Annabelle filled the teapot with hot water to warm it and watched the steam rise from the kettle. It was a new model electric jug. Dad had bought it last year, as soon as it came on the market, just like he'd bought the new Sunbeam mixmaster he expected her to use, and the new radiogram with its honey veneer top, and the new upright vacuum cleaner for Mrs Hester. The mixmaster was gathering dust on the bench. Annabelle hated cooking. She reckoned she'd hate housework if she got married, just as much as she'd hate the bank.

Ned Halloran fell into his chair with a sigh and reached for a sandwich.

'She's a crook old girl, that Ford of Harrison's,' he told Bernie. 'They've run it till it hardly croaks. I reckon if they had a mule they'd flog that to death too.' He bit into his sandwich. The soft white bread sank under his lips and the crisp crust crackled onto his overalls.

Annabelle poured the tea: strong and black for her father, white and weak for her and Bernie, three spoons of sugar for all of them.

'Hey Dad, is it okay if we go out to Aunty Mug's this afternoon? She's expecting us.'

Halloran took another bite of his sandwich, then reached over for more pepper. He looked up at Bernie. 'I thought you might like to give me a hand in the workshop this afternoon,' he said to Bernie. 'Lend a hand to drop the Ford gearbox. Might be interesting. She's a cow of a job that one.'

Bernie looked up cautiously. 'I'd rather go out to Aunty Mug's,' he said.

'You can't always be gallivanting out there,' said Ned Halloran.

'We don't gallivant,' said Annabelle. 'We give Aunty Mug a hand. She's helped us enough.'

'I'd be the last to deny that. But there's enough here to keep you busy, if that's what you want,' said Halloran. 'Most of the boys in town'd give their eye teeth to be under the hoist with me Saturday afternoons. Not mooching down to a rundown stables. I don't know what you see in it. I couldn't wait to be shut of the old place myself.'

'I like it out there.' Bernie shot a look at Annabelle. 'Dad, I've been meaning to talk to you. To tell you. I don't want to be a mechanic.'

Halloran took another bite of sandwich. He looked at Bernie thoughtfully.

'What do you want to do then? Carpenter? Shop fitter? Electrician? How about a plumber? I could get you an apprenticeship with Curly

Morrison if you want one. It's a good trade.'

'I want to go to agricultural college. Then I want to work the farm with Aunty Mug.'

'And I want to be a vet,' said Annabelle.

Their father put his sandwich down. He looked at them. Then he picked it up again. A slice of beetroot slipped onto the plate and he stuffed it back again.

'No,' he said.

'Why not?' demanded Annabelle.

'Because I say so.'

'That's not enough,' said Annabelle. 'Why shouldn't we do what we want to do?'

'Because that's not enough in this world,' said their father. 'Doing what you want to ...' He shook his head. 'I'm saying this for your own good, kids. Good grief, that's what I slave my guts out every day for, for you lot. So you won't have to do it the hard way, like I did. Like your Uncle Ron. Like Maureen, for that matter, slaving away on that place and never making half a life for herself, nothing but a kitchen full of animals instead of a family of her own.'

'That's what Aunty Mug likes,' said Annabelle. 'She wouldn't have it any other way. And Uncle Ron died in the war before we were born.'

'He did. He died up in New Guinea. He

thought he'd stay at school too. He was going to
be a teacher. He didn't like horse on his boots
any more than I did. So I left school and went to
work to help keep him, shovelling out loaves of
bread down at the baker's at four in the morning. I went to night classes and did my apprenticeship, and he went to teachers college, and
what do you think it got him? Not even
tuppence ha'penny. Because the depression came
and there wasn't work for anyone, and it broke
his heart. At least I could pick up a bit of work,
I had my trade, I was safe. But not your Uncle
Ron. He hardly had a decent job till war broke
out and he joined up.'

'But there isn't a depression now,' said
Bernie.

'That's not to say there won't be. And when
it comes, I want you to be safe. The both of you.
I don't want you breaking your heart like Ron. I
want you settled in a trade with a decent family
business under you. I don't want you' — to
Annabelle — 'working till you die, like your
mother. She kept this business going for me in
the war, with only old Jacko to help her when I
was in the Middle East and it broke her, too, it
broke her strength. It breaks my heart sometimes to think I've got the money now and it's
too late to give her any of the things she'd have

liked. I want to see my daughter with clean hands, I want her in a job that'll give her a pay packet at the end of the week and no sweat to get it, not breaking her heart and her back in a man's world, trying to make her way.'

He stood up. The children were silent.

'You go out to Maureen's if you want to. But you think about what I said. Okay?'

'Okay, Dad,' said Annabelle quietly.

Ned Halloran picked up his hat. His hands were stained with grease and oil, not just on the surface but deep between the nails and in cracks along the palm. He looked at Annabelle and Bernie. 'You're good kids,' he said. 'Don't ever think I don't think so. But you don't know how tough life can be yet. You don't know what it can do to you.' He put his hand in his pocket. 'Here, look, how about a couple of shillings to go down to the matinee at the Odeon? You could see the serial and the cartoons. Someone was telling me there's a new Doris Day film on. Get a packet of Minties or an ice-cream or something.'

Annabelle shook her head. 'Thanks, Dad. But we said we'd go out to Aunty Mug's.'

Ned Halloran nodded. 'I'll see you at dinner then,' he said. 'If I'm called out, Mrs Hester's made a stew. It just needs heating. I'll see you later.'

Bernie and Annabelle were quiet. Annabelle got up and began to clear the dishes, wiping the scraps into the bucket for Mrs Hester's chooks.

'What do you think?' she asked Bernie.

'I don't know,' answered Bernie. 'I suppose he's right. But he just doesn't understand.'

'No, he doesn't,' said Annabelle. 'He doesn't realise. He fought to get where he is, and Aunty Mug fought for what she wants. He doesn't realise that maybe we can fight too.'

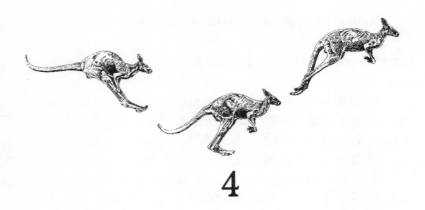

4

The bicycles sped down the road to the farm, new Malvern Stars, shiny as freshly minted halfpennies, their wheels flashing in the sun, past Anderson's shearing shed with the electricity poles for the new plant he had just put in; past the old Collins hayshed that never quite fell down; past Stan Vujic on his new tractor, ploughing up his paddock for a field of oats, the dust sifting through the air like falling icing sugar. Old fences, new fences, wooden gates, and new shiny steel, till they came to the sagging posts that marked the Redgate boundary.

'Aunty Mug needs some new fences,' said Bernie.

'I don't suppose she can afford to get anyone to do it,' said Annabelle. 'She can't do it by herself.'

'Don't say that to Aunty Mug.'

'Of course not.'

'If we were older, we could do them for her.'

'How long would it be before you finished agricultural college?' asked Annabelle.

Bernie counted. 'About twelve years,' he calculated.

'I don't think they'll stand up that long,' said Annabelle.

Bernie nodded. 'I wonder, will they still give us the prize money if Fred wins the Cup? Even if he isn't a horse?'

'I don't know,' said Annabelle. 'They didn't give us the prize money at the gymkhana.'

'That's because they didn't realise Fred was meant to be in the race. They won't make that mistake if we can get him in the Cup.'

'If we had piles of money, we could stay at school as long as we liked.'

'Dad could still say no.'

'We could come and live with Aunty Mug then. She could adopt us.'

Bernie thought. 'It sort of wouldn't be fair to Dad. He doesn't have much time, but I think he'd miss us. We're all the family he's got. Besides, I don't think I want to.'

'I don't want to, either,' said Annabelle. 'I just wish he'd see our side of it.'

They rode up the track, skirting the ruts and the tussocks that grew from the middle.

Aunty Mug was in the yard, trimming Sampson's feet. He whinnied at the sight of them.

'You'll get your apple when I've finished, you old fool,' said Aunty Mug.

'Need a hand, Aunty Mug?'

Aunty Mug shook her head. 'This is the last. Give him an apple or two, will you? I want to go get Darkie. I was out on him earlier, out along the top boundary, and he could do with a good brush down.'

The geese gargled from the orchard, announcing visitors. A car drew up in the yard. It was an FJ Holden, last year's model, not like Aunty Mug's old rattler. Bernie looked at it admiringly. It shone even under its coat of dust. The door opened and Dan Coates got out. He was wearing his go-to-town clothes, his good green sports coat and dark akubra hat. There was a portable wireless on the front seat, whispering its results: '. . . *race three Melbourne and the numbers are official now, number six Lockcutter, ridden by V. Hughes, number three Bog Oak . . .*'

Dan Coates nodded to Annabelle and Bernie.

'I'm looking for your Aunty,' he said. 'She anywhere about?'

Bernie nodded. 'She'll be back in a minute. She's gone to get Darkie. She was out in the hills with him earlier and wants to brush him down.'

Dan slammed the car door behind him. Sampson snickered, startled. "Thunder and forked lightning,' he swore. 'Darkie? Not that rogue horse. That fool of a woman. She'll kill herself. Why can't she accept her age?'

'Are you talking about me, Dan Coates?' It was Aunty Mug, coming round the side of the shed.

Dan looked at her in relief. 'Maureen, these kids told me you were exercising Darkie.'

'So I was,' said Aunty Mug. 'I tired him out. Any objections, Daniel Coates?'

'Maureen, you're not getting any younger.'

'Neither's Darkie. I'm not in my dotage, Dan Coates, even if you are. He's going to be a good horse. You were a fool not to snap him up at the sale. If I don't take him in hand now, he'll be no good at all. Did you come for anything special, or just to criticise my horsemanship?'

'You've got skill, all right,' said Dan Coates. 'Just no sense to go with it. I just called by in a neighbourly way to say hello. That's all.'

Aunty Mug put her hands on her hips. 'Now you've said it,' she said. 'And if you think I'm going to waste my day making you a cup of tea,

you can forget it. I've got work to do, even if you haven't.'

'I should have brought a thermos,' said Dan Coates. 'That's the only way a bloke'd get a cup of tea around here.'

'Good idea, said Aunty Mug. 'You do that next time and I'll have a cup too. You can bring a packet of Iced Vo Vos with you. Fred and I like Iced Vo Vos.'

Dan Coates got back in his car. He didn't quite slam the door.

'*Stand by now, and the placings are, number two Hermit Boy, ridden by . . .*' whispered his wireless.

Dan Coates wound the window down. He looked at Aunty Mug and raised his eyebrows. 'By the way, I'm off to Flemington next Saturday. I can give you a lift if you'd like one.'

Aunty Mug grinned. 'Flemington? For that I'd trust even your driving.'

Dan Coates grinned back. 'That's my Maureen. I'll pick you up at eight-thirty then. We'll have lunch on the way.' He revved the engine. The car slid down the drive, manoeuvring around the potholes.

Aunty Mug watched it go.

'If I was as rude as that to someone,' said

Annabelle, 'Dad would scrub my mouth out with soap.'

'He'd be right,' said Aunty Mug. She picked up the shovel by the wall. 'I've been slinging off at Dan Coates for nearly forty years, since he stuck his ruler up my bra strap in school and twanged it like a catapult. The whole class heard it. I was too embarrassed to wear a bra for weeks. I snuck into the boys cloakroom next day and stuck a yabby in his sports shorts. You could hear him scream across the oval. He never proved I did it, either. It's too late to stop squabbling now. Come on. You two muck out Sampson's stall for me while I do Darkie, then we'll have a cuppa.'

'Aunty Mug!' cried Annabelle. 'What about Fred and the Melbourne Cup? We've been waiting all week!'

Aunty Mug smiled. 'Oh, that. It was a good idea. It was fun seeing him bound past those smart alecs on their horses. But I can't see it working. There's just no way to enter him.'

'What?' cried Bernie.

'You can't mean it?' demanded Annabelle. 'We got him in the gymkhana.'

'The Melbourne Cup's not like the Bradley's Bluff gymkhana,' said Aunty Mug. 'They just don't let anything with four legs and a tail run in the Cup. Places in the Cup are rare as hen's teeth. There may be nothing in the regulations to say that a Melbourne Cup winner has to be a horse — but I can't see them accepting a starter that isn't. There's just no way we can enter him without a proper horse-like background. It would have been fun, but there it is.'

'Aunty Mug, you can't give up. We've had an idea.'

'We've been thinking about it all week, in case you didn't come up with a loophole,' said Bernie.

'Can't we smuggle him in?' asked Annabelle.

'Smuggle in a kangaroo? We'd never do it!'

'You said you never gave up on anything. You said you always win in the end, if you really want something. You just have to keep trying.'

'What would we do when we did get him in?'

'Let him jump the rails! He could catch them up! I know he could!'

Aunty Mug shook her head. 'You've never been to Flemington on Cup day,' she said. 'There's no way you could get a mouse up to the rails, much less a kangaroo.'

'At least let's give it a go!' cried Annabelle.

'You can't give up on the idea just like that!' insisted Bernie.

Aunty Mug looked at them. She grinned. 'You two are as bad as I am,' she said.

'You're the one who taught us,' said Bernie. 'If you want something, fight for it.'

Aunty Mug put down the shovel. 'Come on. Let's put the billy on. Let's think about this together.'

The wireless was still on in the kitchen, announcing the afternoon's races to Harold in his sack and Pig Iron Bob, with the kettle keeping hot on the edge of the fuel stove: '. . . *and they're coming into the straight now, it's Hobson's Choice leading the field, followed by Sweet Starling, and they're rounding the turn . . .*'

'Rounding the turn!' yelled Pig Iron Bob, spitting sunflower seeds onto the carpet.

Aunty Mug took off her gumboots at the door. The children followed her. The kitchen smelt of old soot and damp kangaroo.

'Boxed in at the rails! Boxed in at the rails!' welcomed Pig Iron Bob, stretching his neck out of his cage so they could scratch it.

Fred met them at the kitchen door. He had been sleeping in the sun and his coat looked warm and soft. There were bits of dried grass in the fluff of his stomach.

'Aaaagh?'

'Yes,' said Aunty Mug, 'you can have some afternoon tea too. Come on in, you great big sook. You can have your bread and milk.'

The kitchen was hot from the stove. Harold stuck his head out of his sack and gave a bleat. Aunty Mug filled his milk bottle and put it in a pan of water to warm, then put down a pan of bread and milk for Fred. The wireless burst into the familiar theme for the news: '*Da dah da da da daaaah . . .*'

Aunty Mug turned it down. 'Who'd listen to the news,' she said. 'It's all politics. Reds under the bed and the yellow peril and the DLP. I haven't had time for politics since Doc Evatt.' She rummaged under the bench for the old copper saucepan. 'How about some cocoa? Blossom's giving more milk than Fred and Harold and I can drink.'

Annabelle nodded. Bernie got the cups down from the dresser, carefully choosing saucers that weren't chipped.

'What about if we dressed Fred up?' he asked. 'We could put him in a dress or something and a great big hat, and he could sit in the back seat and go through the turnstiles with us.'

'What about his feet?' demanded Annabelle. 'You can't disguise those.'

'We could all pretend to be kangaroos then,' suggested Bernie. 'We could say we're dressing up for the Cup.'

'It wouldn't work,' said Aunty Mug. 'You'd never get him close enough to the fence. Even if we dressed him up like Lady Muck and the Lady Mayoress put together. The Cup's got crowded since the war.' She tested Harold's milk and picked him up to feed him. Harold sucked her finger, found the bottle and started slurping. He shut his eyes in delight. Aunty Mug stroked him absently. 'If only I had a runner for one of the other races,' she said. 'We could take him in the float. That's the place to get him in, down past the saddling ring. But I haven't had anything of that standard for years.'

'How about a food delivery van?'

'They don't get close enough,' said Aunty Mug. 'Besides, how do we get Fred into a delivery van?'

Fred was dozing on the sacks by the stove. He looked up at his name. 'Aaaagh?'

'He's bored,' said Bernie. 'He wants to go for a run. Could I saddle up old Sampson, Aunty Mug? Then Fred could run with us.'

Aunty Mug was silent. Bernie looked at her, wondering if she'd heard. 'It's no good, is it?' he asked. 'We'll never get him there.'

Aunty Mug looked up. 'I'm thinking,' she said. She patted Harold's ears absently, put him back in his sack, then got up. 'You kids wait here. I've got an idea. Not much of one, but it might work. I'll be back later. Feed Harold, will you, if I'm not back by four? You know where everything is. Don't forget — it's one spoon of egg yolk and a drop of cod liver oil to a cup of milk. You know where everything is if you're hungry yourselves.'

'Where are you going?' asked Annabelle.

'Ask me no questions and I'll tell you no lies. I'll let you now if it works,' said Aunty Mug. 'Now, where's my hat? No, not that one. I want my good black felt with the feathers. I might just put a skirt on too, while I'm about it. In an enterprise like this, little things make all the difference.' She grinned. 'If I hadn't used my last tube before the war, I'd put on lipstick.' She hurried off.

'Into the straight! Into the straight!' yelled Pig Iron Bob from the corner of the kitchen, knocking over his water dish so it dripped onto the floor.

Annabelle and Bernie watched the car rattle down the driveway. The geese shrieked as it passed. The tall casuarinas swayed above the dust cloud. Fred chased the car lazily halfway down, then loped back to the children, disappointed that it hadn't gone fast enough for a decent run.

Bernie scratched his tan red stomach. Fred stretched happily, leaning back on his tail. 'Sorry. Fred. She's thinking about something else. Come on. I'll get on Sampson and give you a really good run for a while.'

'I'll ring the garage,' said Annabelle. 'Better led Dad know we mightn't be back till late.' She crossed to the phone and turned the handle, then picked up the receiver. The switchboard answered.

'Bradley's Bluff.'

'Helen? It's Annabelle here. Could you put me through to Dad at the garage please?'

'Sure thing, love, but you won't find him there. I saw the repair truck go out just half an hour ago on the road to Wilson's Crossing, and I haven't seen it come back again. How about I give him a buzz for you later? You out at Redgate?'

'Yes. I just wanted to tell him we mightn't be back for dinner.'

'I thought that was you and Bernie on your bicycles earlier,' said Helen on the switchboard. 'I said to Mum at the time, they'll be going out to see their aunty, that's what they'll be doing.'

There was pause on the line. 'Mum says to say hello to your aunty and ask her if she's got a tip for the three-thirty.'

'Aunty Mug's not here just at the moment. But I'll ask her when she comes in,' said Annabelle. 'Thanks very much, Helen. See you later.'

It was a long afternoon. Bernie caught Sampson and rode him up to the top hill, where the old red gums leant against the sky. Fred pounded the ground around them, circling the cantering horses, making sharp dashes in front and coming back to bark them on. From the hill you could see the long paddocks with grass like old men's stubble, and the blue-green fringe of bush beyond. You could see the road to town, too, snaking through the paddocks like a dusty creek, but there was no sign of Aunty Mug.

In the middle of the afternoon, the phone rang. Annabelle picked it up. It was her father. 'Oh, hi Dad,' she said. 'I just wanted to let you know we mightn't be back till late. Is that okay?'

Her father sounded tired on the other end. 'That's okay, love. The way things are going here, I won't be finished till late anyway. I've had three calls already today and I haven't touched McGregor's radiator yet. The sooner your brother gets his mechanic's ticket, the better.'

Annabelle put the phone down quietly. She looked out the window at the thin green line of trees against the blue. She wondered if Bernie would ever be happy with his head under the body of a car, smelling grease instead of paddocks. She wondered how she'd stand the four walls of a bank every day, handling pens and paper, passbooks and adding machines, instead of the warm fur of animals.

The shadows lengthened. Pig Iron Bob dozed on the verandah rail and left white droppings on the floor. Annabelle picked strawberries in the old wild beds under the lichened apple trees planted by her great-grandmother last century, and hunted for eggs in the hay where the chooks preferred to lay, ignoring the proper laying boxes in their yard. Four o'clock came without the rattle of the Holden down the track. Annabelle fed Harold and took him out to wet, and changed the lining of his sack. At six, Bernie locked up the chooks and Jeremiah and Lamentations and their horde, and milked Blossom. They watched the horses bend to eat in the cool of dusk.

'I'd better ring Dad again,' said Annabelle.

THE ROO THAT WON THE MELBOURNE CUP

'Say we're spending the night. We'll never get back before dark now.'

'Aunty Mug might drive us back.'

'We'd have to leave our bikes though, so we couldn't get back here unless Dad had time to give us a lift.'

Bernie nodded. 'Do you think she's all right? You don't suppose there's been an accident?'

'To Aunty Mug? Accidents never happen to Aunty Mug. She wouldn't let them.'

The kitchen clock chimed seven o'clock. Bernie put the wireless on for the news and weather. The static crackled and the voice was faint. '. . . *and it's Spruso for your hair,*' it sang.

'Must be a storm around. That clock's fast,' said Bernie.

'Aunty Mug likes it fast,' said Annabelle. 'She says no-one's going to say she's behind the times.'

Annabelle took some chops out of the meat safe and put them on to cook in the big black frypan, with potatoes and carrots and cabbage from the garden.

Bernie took the plates from the dresser, old rose-patterned plates with chips and scratches that Aunty Mug loved and refused to replace, and set the cutlery on the oilcloth. There was a scratching at the door. 'Aaaagh!' Heavy feet bounded round the house and back again, then came another scratch and growl.

'It's Fred,' said Bernie. 'He wants his dinner.'

Fred loped slowly into the kitchen. His nose twitched as he looked around. His long feet were muddy with leaf mould from jumping through the garden. 'She's gone out, you silly roo,' said Annabelle. 'Here, what do you want? There's bread and apple or cabbage leaves. I'd better wash your milk pan out, or you'll get sick.'

Fred took the bread in both paws. He nibbled delicately. The crumbs spilled over his chest and onto the floor. His nose twitched towards the griller.

'No you don't, you messy macropod. That's our dinner. Kangaroos don't eat chops.'

'They might,' said Fred's eyes. Suddenly his ears perked up, backwards, forwards, then finally towards the drive. He gave his bark, 'Aaaagh', and headed for the door. It swung open as he pushed it.

'She's on the home run!' yelled Pig Iron Bob, woken by the noise, stretching his wings so wide that the cage rocked and spilt seed out the sides.

Annabelle and Bernie followed Fred. It was

cold outside, the spring breeze whistling up with the darkness. The night brought scents of horses from the paddocks, warm soil and the hint of gums from the hills. They could hear the Holden now, stuttering up the drive. They could see the flash of Fred's tail in the headlights as he pounded down to meet it, then raced it back, loping up the corrugated drive as if it were the open plains.

The old car put on speed, bouncing in the potholes. Fred loped gracefully in the beams of light. He sped past the children into the yard, wheeled easily, then bounded slowly back. The car pulled up with a squeak of old brakes.

Aunty Mug got out. She looked tired, but triumphant as she stepped into the house. Her velvet hat was crooked. 'I clocked him at 40 miles an hour tonight,' she said. 'They'll never touch him.'

'You mean?' cried Annabelle.

Aunty Mug nodded. 'We're in!' she said. 'I've arranged it all. Dan Coates'll take us in his double horse box. He'll smuggle us in. He's got a runner in the second race at Flemington.'

'But why?' said Annabelle. 'How on earth did you get him to agree? What if he gets caught? Why would he do a thing like that?'

Aunty Mug smiled. 'I promised him I'd

marry him if we won,' she said simply.

'And they're racing!' screamed Pig Iron Bob, triumphant on the windowsill.

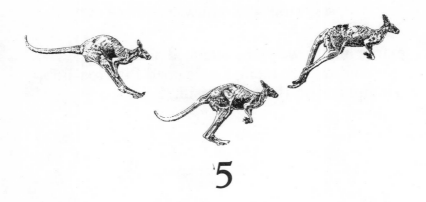

5

The trailer swayed behind Dan Coates' truck. Ronnie Bates, Dan's head groom, was driving. The truck smelt of manure and exhaust fumes. In the next partition, Irish Lad whinnied uneasily. Dan's soft voice reassured him. There was silence, except for the noise of the road beneath them.

'I think I'm going to be sick,' said Annabelle. She looked down at her new pointed black shoes under the froth of her rope petticoats. She hoped she'd make it out the door in time if she was. Her dress was new, too, and her long white socks. Dad had taken her shopping when they told her Dan Coates was taking them down to the Cup. There'd been no mention of roo smuggling. Annabelle wondered what he'd say when he found out. She felt guilty at the thought of her father serving all the Cup day customers by himself at the bowser in the

74

middle of the hot concrete while they had a day in town. The small square garage with its taller workshop and tiny patch of lawn seemed a long way away.

'Well, you can't be sick,' said Aunty Mug. 'You might wake up Fred.'

'He's slept a long time,' said Bernie.

'It's the motion of the truck,' explained Aunty Mug. 'Besides, he's getting older. Roos like the night more than the day.'

Aunty Mug looked hot and excited. She had a drab coat over her go-to-the-races dress to keep it clean, and her good fox furs were draped over a bale of hay. She reached up to Harold's hessian sack on the wall and stroked him absently. Bernie peered over the edge of the horse box at the flat Melbourne plains sailing by. They were dry and uninteresting after the bush at home. The day to come would be more exciting. Even if they didn't win, there was still the Cup, the visit to Melbourne and his new black stovepipe pants and Sinatra-red socks. He touched his hair carefully. It was still in place. He'd borrowed Dad's Spruso early this morning when they left, and poured on Californian Poppy. His hair felt like patent leather. He hoped it would last the day.

Gravel roads gave way to bitumen, potholes

disappeared on the smoother roads nearer Melbourne. There was more traffic now. Horns blared around them and they could hear the clatter of trams. The trailer lurched and hiccoughed as it stopped for the traffic lights.

'I wish we could look out properly,' said Annabelle. 'It's exciting.'

They ate sandwiches and drank lemonade from the old tin esky. Dan Coates put his head through the partition and joined them. He'd turned on the wireless to hear the scratchings and it muttered behind him.

'I must be crazy,' he said. 'Crazy as a hare in springtime.'

'You always were,' said Aunty Mug. 'Remember when you put the rabbit in the teacher's desk, and old man Boskins picked up one of its pellets by mistake and thought it was a stub of brown chalk, and tried to use it on the blackboard? I like a man who takes a risk.'

Dan Coates snorted. 'None of your flattery, Maureen. It was your idea, anyway. Who was it found the rabbit? I was ten years old then. I should have learned more sense by now than to listen to you. Just remember, keep down behind the hay bales as we go in. Luckily they know me.'

'Don't skite,' said Aunty Mug.

'I am crazy,' said Dan. He looked at Harold's sack, hung on a nail on the wall. 'What did you bring that wombat for, anyway? Isn't one marsupial enough for the day?'

'Who else would feed him while I'm gone?' demanded Aunty Mug. 'He doesn't take up much room. Which reminds me. Pass him down. It's tucker time. You tend to your animals, Daniel Coates, and I'll tend to mine.'

'Huh!' snorted Dan, as he went back to Irish Lad.

'. . . *and next we'll be having a look at the situation at Flemington, race number four today and the scratchings are Redwood Lass, My Jean, Highnose Prince and Shooting Star . . .*' announced the wireless.

Flemington was noisy. The ground was a sea of horse boxes. Clouds of hats and silks floated in the distance. The sun gleamed on the rounded curves of black Rolls-Royces, grey Daimlers, racey E-type Jags in British racing reds and greens, brand new Holdens, elderly Vauxhalls, Austins. The air smelt of horses and cars and perfume. There were cries from the bookies, barks from the loudspeakers, the song of bright chatter from the crowd. It was another world, as different from a country race meeting as the sea from the bush.

'All of Melbourne must be here!' whispered Annabelle.

'All of Australia,' said Bernie as the trailer bumped over to the stalls. They crouched behind the hay bales and listened to the noises of people, stamping horses, loudspeakers. Dan and Ronnie led Irish Lad out and shut the door. The children stood up, safe from view again. They peeped over the bales to watch him. Dan looked different now, his old overalls off, in his good three-piece pin-striped suit and his grey Borsalino hat with hair-oil stains round its black band.

'He's sort of handsome,' whispered Annabelle.

'Tell that to Aunty Mug,' Bernie whispered back.

Irish Lad whinnied at the smell of the other horses and the excitement in the air. There was the sound of last-minute currying from the stables, the clang of water buckets, the whisper of hay around restless horses.

'Horses can sense it,' said Aunty Mug. 'You'd have to be half dead not to feel the thrill on a day like this. Hey, what do you think you're up to, Fred?'

'He wants to get out,' said Bernie.

'I think he's following Irish Lad,' said Annabelle.

'Well, have some bread instead. Sit down, you hairy fool. I know it's exciting, but you have to wait. Your race isn't for ages yet.'

'Why did we have to get here so early?' asked Annabelle. 'Not that I mind. It's exciting.'

'Got to give Irish Lad the chance to settle down before his race,' said Aunty Mug. 'Get him a bit used to the place. Horses can sense the atmosphere. They get excited too. A good horse knows it's there to win. No, Fred, that's all you're getting. Settle down and I'll give your neck a scratch.'

'Aaaagh,' said Fred.

There was a tapping on the side of the trailer. Dan Coates was back. 'You kids like to come for a walk for a while? I've left Ronnie with the Lad. No sense staying cooped up till the race.'

Bernie and Annabelle glanced at Aunty Mug. She nodded. 'You two go off,' she told them. 'Fred'll be fine here with me.'

They stepped out into the lane by the stables. It was wet with fresh hosing and scattered with straw. The tall pale piles of manure steamed from grain-fed horses.

'Even the horses smell different,' said Annabelle. 'Like they've been washed.'

'Well, they have,' said Dan. 'And brushed and shined and plaited. I spent an hour just on the Lad's hooves yesterday. The whole world's watching today. It'll be in movie houses in Sydney by this afternoon and all over the world in a few days.'

They were out in the crowd now, beyond the stables and the smell of horse sweat, into the world of spectators and high heeled shoes. The ground was already white with betting tickets, scattered like snow over the green of the grass, and thick with cigarette butts, pie bags and lolly papers.

'Even the track is green,' said Annabelle in wonder. 'They must water it. Look at those roses! There must be hundreds of them. I never thought a track could be so pretty.'

Bernie looked around. His new trousers didn't feel half as smart here. He felt his hair carefully to make sure it was still in place. 'What's that place over there? With all the top hats and grey suits,' he asked.

'Members enclosure,' said Dan. 'That's for the cream of society.'

'Are you a member, Mr Coates?' said Annabelle.

THE ROO THAT WON THE MELBOURNE CUP

Dan grinned. 'No, pet. I'm here for the horses, not the champagne.'

'Look at those dresses,' went on Annabelle in awe. 'That woman over there must be wearing a dozen petticoats.'

'Hey, look,' whispered Bernie. 'Blue hair!'

'Shh,' said Dan, smiling. 'Blue hair's the fashion of the fifties. I saw a woman with green at the Caulfield. Where to now, kids? Do you just want to look around? How about a lemonade? How about putting a bet on? You've got to put a bet on the Cup. Come on, I'll shout you.'

Annabelle shook her head, indignant. 'How can we? Fred's the one that's going to win the Cup. And we can't bet on him because he isn't entered.'

Dan sighed. 'Look kids, I know you love your aunty. She's a wonderful woman. A woman in a thousand. I love her too. She's got you into this just like she got me. But don't you be too disappointed if it doesn't come off. All right?'

Bernie didn't reply. Annabelle looked Dan in the eye. 'Fred is going to win,' she stated.

Dan sighed again. 'You're as bad as she is,' he said. 'All right, I give in. Of course Fred's going to win. How about a bet on the next race, then? I'll put five shillings for both of you on Irish Lad to win.'

Annabelle smiled at him. 'Thank you very much, Mr Coates. But could you back him for a place instead?'

'A place!' repeated Dan.

Annabelle nodded. 'Aunty Mug says he hasn't got the temper for a winner. She says he likes to have another horse's tail where he can see it. But she says he's got a good chance for second or third.'

Dan laughed. 'You and your blooming aunt. She could be right at that. But on a day like this, it doesn't matter. It's worth it just to be part of the Cup.'

They wandered over to the bookies' ring. Umbrellas rose like toadstools, bookies in white Panama hats and striped suits with chalk dust at their wrists shouted from their platforms.

'Five to one the field!'

'Fifty each way on number nine!'

'Evens! That's what I'm offering! Evens to the bloke at the back.'

Behind them the pencillers scribbled in their books and the bagmen with white canvas bags and patent leather shoes thrust fistfuls of change at the customers. Old pound notes were pulled from pockets; shillings and sixpences gleamed in the sun. Crowds milled before each umbrella, shopping for the best odds: women in bright lipstick and pastel dresses, women in lampshade hats and white netting gloves, men in wide-shouldered suits with skinny legs, tweed suits, striped suits and sports coats, the possum faced urgers listening for their tips in thin-brimmed hats of chequered tweed.

'One hundred on number six!'

'You're on!'

'Give you three a place on number four!'

'Come on,' said Bernie. 'We'd better be getting back. Aunty Mug might need a hand with Fred.'

They walked back up to the trailer. Horses stepped past them, heads high, with silken coats that shone like polished metal, their noses reaching for the sky.

'They know they're special, don't they?' whispered Annabelle. The sun and the crowd were so bright, the noise of the speakers and the cries behind them were so loud, her head was beginning to ache.

'They are special,' said Dan. 'You've got to be special to run with half Australia watching you. There'll be millions of people listening to this race. A five shilling bet and each of them feels they own the track.'

Fred was asleep when they got back. He looked small and scruffy after the golden horses.

Aunty Mug looked different from the smart city women in their pastel dresses and their hats.

'Thank you very much, Mr Coates,' said Annabelle politely. She wished her headache would go away.

'A pleasure,' said Dan. 'See you after the race, Maureen.' He paused. 'Good luck.'

'Good luck, Dan,' said Aunty Mug. 'Here, give us a kiss for luck.' She poked her head out of the trailer.

Dan went back to the stables to check on Irish Lad. Aunty Mug leant against the trailer wall, watching Fred. She looked flushed and hot and excited. The children sat beside her. They spoke in whispers.

'It's wonderful, Aunty Mug,' said Annabelle. 'So many people. And the dresses!'

'They're spending pounds,' whispered Bernie. 'The ground's thick with betting tickets. Everyone looks so rich!'

'It's the grandest day of the year,' said Aunty Mug. 'It's the one day you get dressed up for. When would I ever wear lipstick except to the Melbourne Cup?' She proudly showed them a new tube in her handbag. 'It's called Crimson Flash,' she said. 'I saw the label and I thought of Fred. He's our brown and fluffy flash. Aren't you Fred?'

'Aaaagh,' said Fred sleepily, waking up. Aunty Mug scratched his chest idly with the toe of her shoe.

'Now, I'll have roo hairs all over my nylons,' she complained. 'Never mind. Now, remember the plan,' she ordered. 'We make a dash for it ten minutes before the race. I go first. I'll tell them I'm joining Dan down in the saddling ring. I'll get as close to the race as I can. Then you let Fred out. Just don't panic, whatever happens. There'll be a fuss. Just remember, Fred's big enough to get through anywhere. Just stay with him down to the saddling ring. As soon as he hears my whistle, he'll be right. He'll run through the crowd and join me at the ring. If anyone tries to stop him, he'll just jump over them. As soon as he sees those horses run, he'll be over the fence and after them. Just you keep running. It's still a long way to the track from here.'

Bernie shook his head. 'There's so many more people than I thought,' he said. 'It's all so much bigger. Fred looks awfully small compared to some of those horses.'

'I've got a headache,' said Annabelle.

'It'll go,' said Aunty Mug. 'It's the waiting.'

'I'm scared,' admitted Annabelle.

'So am I,' said Aunty Mug.

'Aaaagh,' said Fred.

Aunty Mug scratched his ears. 'You'll be right,' she said.

Ten past two, twenty past two. Aunty Mug slipped off her coat, straightened her hat, picked the straw out of her fox furs and slipped on her toe-peeper shoes. 'Here, you keep my watch. Don't lose it, whatever you do,' she said. 'Pass me my lizard handbag and I'll be off. Now, you remember the plan? Just keep your eye on the time and you'll be right.'

Twenty-three past two. Aunty Mug put her hands round Fred's shoulders. 'I want you to listen, Fred. There'll be lots of horses out there. More horses than you've ever seen before. They'll be running like the wind and their feet'll sound like thunder. They're all bigger than you and their legs are longer. But I want you to remember something. This is your country, Fred. You were here before the first horse put its hoof on Australian soil. The ground under your feet is your ground. Those big feet of yours were born to run on it.

'Those horses out there think this is their day, Melbourne Cup day. But you're going to show them, Fred. This is still your country. You show them, Fred. You get out there and claim the world. You go and win.'

Fred look at Aunty Mug, puzzled. 'Aaaagh,' he said.

Aunty Mug scratched his ears. 'You're a winner, Fred. Whatever happens today, whatever happens in that race, you're still a winner.'

She touched Bernie's shoulder lightly, touched Annabelle's cheek. 'This is it,' she said. 'Good luck, kids.'

Twenty-five past two. Aunty Mug slipped out of the box. Fred twitched his nose and started to follow her. Bernie held him back.

'Not yet, boy. Soon.'

Half-past two. Twenty-five to three.

'Do you think Aunty Mug's down at the rails by now?' whispered Annabelle. 'What if she can't get a place? What if Fred can't get through to her? There seem to be an awful lot of people out there.'

Bernie shook his head. 'Things can't go wrong now. They can't. We've got so close. How's your headache?'

'Gone,' whispered Annabelle.

Fred was restless. He made small hops around the trailer.

The second hand slipped slowly round the watch face. Twenty to three. 'Let's go!' whispered Bernie. 'Come on, Fred. Now!'

Out of the box. Horses paced past, gleaming

and braided. Jockeys flashed by in bright thin silk. A stable lad walking past with a bucket in each hand pointed and stared.

'Hey, what do you lot think you're doing?'

'Just giving the roo a stretch,' said Annabelle airily.

'Quickly,' muttered Bernie. 'Before we're stopped. Down this way, Aunty Mug said.'

Fred sniffed the air, curious, at home among the horses. He sniffed a pile of droppings, tasted some fallen wheat, then followed the children.

'. . . *and the starting prices for the Melbourne Cup* . . .' droned the loudspeaker overhead '. . . *Eglantine has shortened to evens . . . Bold as Brass is down to tens . . . Harvest Home has blown out to one hundred . . .*'

'Hey! What's going on over there? You there, what do you think you're doing?'

'Hoy! You kids with the roo!'

'Time to start running!' whispered Bernie.

They ran from the stable area, over the ground stamped muddy by horse hooves and straw. Fred bounded behind them. They were out in the open now, heads turning. The smell of the stables, fresh droppings, fresh sweat, freshly hosed cobbles, was behind them. They could smell the crowd smells, tweed coats and boots and the scents of hats and perfume, over the smells of horse and hay.

'Hey look! What is it?'

'Kangaroo! There's a kangaroo!'

'Kangaroo! Someone's brought a kangaroo!'

'Let's get going!' muttered Bernie.

Footsteps were running behind them, someone was yelling at them. 'You kids! Hey, you kids! Stop! What do you think you're doing?'

'There's the tunnel!' yelled Bernie to Annabelle. 'That way! Follow, Fred, follow!'

'Aaaagh!' cried Fred, excited already.

Up above them, speakers crackled: '. . . *and the scratchings are Bright Lass . . .*'

They picked up speed. Fred loped along happily. He'd been bored till now. He always liked a chase. Lots of people, lots of horses. This was fun.

'Hey, what do you think you're doing?'

'Mavis, do you see what I see . . . ?'

'Hoy, someone! Catch that roo!'

Down the tunnel to the saddling ring. Horses cantered out of the way, their eyes rolling. Fred bounded in front of them, brushing past a nervous horse, circled round and came back behind them.

'Heel, Fred! Heel!'

'He doesn't understand!' panted Annabelle. 'Don't worry. He'll stay close.'

'Hey, watch it, you kids! Where do you think you're going?'

'What is this, a flaming circus?'

'Hey, someone, grab that roo!'

Out of the tunnel. They were running hard now, panting, ducking between people, hoping to get past them before they realised what was happening. Fred hopped easily behind. The crowd was different here, not lads and jockeys and owners in overalls to keep their good clothes clean. This was a well-dressed crowd, ladies in heels and wide-cut skirts and hats with skimpy veils, men in morning dress with bell-toppers and clean-shaven chins, men in tweed suits with flowers in their buttonholes. More shouts and yells.

'It's a roo! A bloody kangaroo!'

'Stone the flaming crows! Look there!'

'Hey, cop this! A roo! Over there! A roo!'

'We'll never make it,' panted Bernie. 'There's too many people. I never guessed it'd be like this.'

The shock was dying down. The crowd was turning purposeful. The people ahead of them knew something was up now.

'Catch them! Catch the roo!'

'Keep running!' screamed Annabelle, dodging a man in grey.

Fred padded at their heels. Someone grabbed his shoulder. Fred cocked his hind leg up. He pushed and was free.

'The monster's torn my shirt!'

'Be careful of that roo! He's savage!'

'The kangaroo! The kangaroo!'

'It's the kids! It's with the kids! Get them! Get them!'

More shouts. 'Catch them! Get hold of them! No, that way you fool!'

A hand grabbed Bernie. He tried to duck, but the hand was too firm.

'No you don't my lad,' said a firm voice.

'Annabelle! Run!' Bernie shouted. 'Keep going! Get Fred to the barrier!'

The speakers muttered up above: '. . . *and the red light's flashing, as they settle down at the barriers. Comanche Prince is playing up . . .*'

'It's starting!' shrieked Bernie. 'Annabelle, the race is starting! Keep going! You've got to get him there!'

Annabelle twisted and ducked. More hands reached out for Fred, and missed.

'Get the girl! The roo's with her! Someone get that girl!'

Horses snorted, sidestepped, reared and

THE ROO THAT WON THE MELBOURNE CUP

whinnied. Annabelle ducked under someone's arm, dodged a hand, ran around a knot of gossipers. Fred loped around her. Her chest was tight. It was hard to breathe. Another hand reached for her, an official lunged. She was caught. She twisted wildly.

'Fred! Keep running! Please, Fred! Run!'

Fred balanced on his tail, wondering. A hand reached out for him. He boxed it away, casually. The speakers boomed above them.

'*And they're racing!*'

'Aunty Mug!' screamed Annabelle, as she tried to escape the hands that held her. 'Fred, please, find Aunty Mug.' Fred blinked, puzzled.

The people around them were listening to the speakers now. There was a last-minute rush towards the ring. Even a kangaroo on the course was less interesting than the running of the Cup. The course was almost silent, the crowd thinned, most people at the rails for the race of the year.

'Please!' pleaded Annabelle to her captor.

'Shush,' said a woman nearby.

'. . . *first to jump is Able Warrior, followed by Red Alert, Eglantine, Bold as Brass badly missed the start, then it's Comanche Prince, Johnnie's Revenge . . .*'

Fred scratched his stomach, confused by the

noise, wondering what game the kids were playing now.

You could almost hear the beat of hooves.
Perhaps you could feel them, vibrating through
the ground. Suddenly the hats and tweeds and
perfume were irrelevant. This was a world of
horses again. The race was the most important
thing in the world. Fred stood alert now, his ears
slowly turning this way and that.

Then came the whistle. It was faint at first,
then louder. Fred heard it. His ears turned
towards the sound. He sniffed the wind.

'Go, Fred, Go!' urged Annabelle.

'What the blazes . . . ' swore the official.

Fred bounded forwards. A cordon of officials blocked his path, hurrying through the
crowd. Fred leapt, they ducked. His tail flashed
over their heads. Someone yelled and he was
gone. Annabelle and her captor watched him go.
The loudspeaker droned overhead.

'*. . . settling down on the back straight we
have Eglantine, Johnnie's Revenge, Red Alert and
Able Warrior, Comanche Prince, Fool's Gold . . .*'

'Now young lady, you come with me. What
on earth do you think you were doing there?
Where did you get that roo?'

'*. . . and Bold as Brass is coming last . . .
coming up to the first turn and it's Johnnie's*'

THE ROO THAT WON THE MELBOURNE CUP

Revenge ahead of Red Alert, Eglantine and Able Warrior . . .'

Annabelle stood shaking, trying to hold back tears. Another official in a short white coat brought Bernie up, holding tightly to his elbow. 'What is all this?' he demanded. 'Where's that kangaroo?'

Annabelle gulped down sobs. 'He'll never make it,' she said. 'We're too late.'

'Who'll never make it? Where's that roo of yours? Do you realise the damage you could have done? There are the most valuable horses in the world here!'

The world was suddenly quieter. The crowd had thinned even more. The loudspeaker boomed loud above them.

'. . . *coming past the barrier for the second time and it's Able Warrior by a length, Comanche Prince, Eglantine on the inside, Fool's Gold, Johnnie's Revenge, Harvest Home, Rebel Fancy and Big Jim . . .*'

'Where did you get that roo? How did you get in here? Where's he gone? Speak up now!'

'. . . *with Bold as Brass trailing the field, and they're coming round the home turn, it's Able Warrior in the lead closely watched by Johnnie's Revenge, Eglantine . . .*'

Annabelle reached for her hanky.

'. . . *Able Warrior still in the lead, Eglantine coming up fast on the inside, then it's Red Alert and a . . . a kangaroo . . . a kangaroo? . . . starve the lizards . . . there's a bloody kangaroo on the track . . . the kangaroo is leading Red Alert by a nose . . . they're coming into the turn now . . . the kangaroo is still there . . .'*

Annabelle turned to Bernie. 'He's on the track! He got there!'

'He must have seen them running! He must have jumped the rail! He got there himself!'

'Fred! Oh, Fred!'

Even the officials were quiet now. You could feel the expectation as thick as syrup in the air. The speakers droned above them. The roar from the ring grew louder.

'Eglantine! Come on, you little beauty!'

'Red Alert!'

'Come on, Able Warrior!'

'Eglantine!'

'Come on, Fred!' yelled Annabelle. 'Move your tail!'

'. . . *coming up to the nine hundred, it's Eglantine up on the inside, Able Warrior then the kangaroo, it's passed Red Alert now, it's coming up fast, coming up on the outside is Rebel Fancy, half a length behind Big Jim, Harvest Home tucked in on the inside . . . it's Eglantine leading by a length with the kangaroo coming up fast, it's passed Able Warrior, followed by Red Alert, Fool's Gold, Comanche Prince, Johnnie's Revenge, Harvest Home, Big Jim and Rebel Fancy . . .'*

'Come on, Fred!' whispered Annabelle.

'You can do it, Fred! You can do it!'

'One more to pass, Fred. Just one more to pass!'

'. . . a shade over four hundred to go, Eglantine is losing ground, it's the kangaroo, the kangaroo is overtaking Eglantine, it's bounding out in front of Eglantine, followed by Able Warrior, Red Alert, Comanche Prince now in front of Fool's Gold, Johnnie's Revenge, Harvest Home . . .'

'Whacko!' yelled Annabelle.

'. . . Sergeant Sam looming up now on the outside in front of Battle Prince, followed by Bold as Brass pulling hard . . .'

'Bernie!'

'He's going to do it! He's going to do it!'

'. . . the kangaroo has kicked away from them now, it's well in the lead . . . Eglantine is pulling up behind, can she make it, can she make it . . .'

The crowd was roaring below them, high-pitched yells and deeper cries, as though it had one voice and no words between them, yelling, cheering, on and on . . .

The official let go of Bernie. He shook his head. He was smiling. Annabelle's captor was listening too.

'. . . *And it's the kangaroo! The kangaroo has won the Melbourne Cup! Then it's Eglantine, Able Warrior, Red Alert . . .*'

'He's done it,' cried Bernie. Annabelle grabbed his hands. They danced around and around the bemused officials.

'He's done it, he's done it, Fred's done it!'

'Good on you, Fred!'

The official was looking at them. 'I think the time has come for explanations,' he said.

Annabelle looked up at him. 'Please, could we find our aunty first? And we need to get Fred. He might be scared. Someone might hurt him.'

'Fred's the kangaroo?' The official grinned. 'Don't you worry about Fred, pet. No-one's going to hurt a Cup winner. Not even when it's a kangaroo.'

Aunty Mug recaptured Fred, down in the winners' enclosure where she'd always longed to be. Her furs hung crooked on her shoulder and she'd lost her hat. Her grin was wider than a river, brighter than sunlight on the water.

'You beauty, Fred! You little beauty. I knew

you'd do it. You ran like a cloud in the wind!
You ran like a stick shooting down a creek in
flood! You ran like a kangaroo! Good on you,
Fred, my darling Fred. You showed them who
was who.'

'Aaaagh,' said Fred.

Fred was excited. He panted. His ears
twitched this way and that. He licked his paws
to cool himself. He sniffed at Aunty Mug's
handbag for the apple she always gave him at the
end of a run.

'Here you are, Fred. A whole one today. Just
for you.'

'Aaaagh,' said Fred, taking his apple in both
paws. The juice ran down his chin and stomach
as he nibbled with his sharp front teeth. Cam-
eras clicked around them.

One of the officials cleared his throat. 'Perhaps if we could take the . . . er . . . animal to a
more private place. We don't want him running
away again.'

'His name's Fred,' declared Aunty Mug, 'and
he can go back to the trailer. Go on kids, take
him back and stay there with him for a while.'
She nodded at the ring of officials. 'There's a
few things I need to sort out.'

'Indeed there are,' the officials agreed solemnly. But they were, the kids could see, awfully near to grinning.

Dan Coates came back to the trailer half an hour later. He was grinning too. Irish Lad had been placed third in the next race.

'Not bad,' said Dan. 'Even if it wasn't the Cup.'

He bought them sarsaparilla and meat pies. Fred sniffed at the crust, tasted and rejected it. He lay on his side and nibbled Irish Lad's hay.

The yard was quiet when Aunty Mug came back. Most of the horses were gone. Aunty Mug looked tired. Her fringe was sticking up and her fox furs trailed from one shoulder. But her grin stretched from ear to ear.

'I promised we'd never do it again,' she said with satisfaction. 'So they let me go. I said it wasn't Dan's fault either. I said I'd argued him into it. They just laughed and said he had their sympathy. No-one in Melbourne's going to prosecute a Cup winner, not on Melbourne Cup day. Besides, the less publicity the better. As for not doing it again — how many Cup winners does a woman need in her lifetime?'

'Eglantine got the Cup,' said Annabelle. 'They said so on the speaker.'

'She'll get the money, too, won't she?' asked Bernie.

'Fair enough,' said Aunty Mug. 'After all, she was in the race from the start. Fred only joined it in the middle.' She grinned at Bernie. 'Don't you worry about money, pet. Your old aunty's got it all sorted out. I've sold my story to the *Women's Weekly*. There'll be enough to repair the fences for a few years yet.' She moved over to Dan.

'Well, you old fool? Don't just stand there like a stuffed mullet! Can I train them or can't I?'

Dan threw his arm around her shoulders. Her fox furs fell off into the hay. Neither of them noticed. 'You're a winner, Maureen. You're crazy as a two bob watch, but you're a winner.'

'Aaaagh,' agreed Fred, watching from a corner. He sniffed the furs and went back to his hay.

'Don't you mind? asked Bernie. 'About not getting the Cup and the money?'

'Mind? On the day I've been in the winners' circle with my very own runner in the Melbourne Cup? You know, I don't think I'll ever mind anything again.'

Dan kissed her. 'You're the only woman who could have done it,' he informed her. 'They'll remember you forever — a trainer so good she could win the Cup with a kangaroo.'

'Aaaagh,' said Fred. He scratched his stomach lazily. He'd had his run for the day. He looked pleased with himself. Let others worry about prize money and cups. Fred had charged a mob of horses galloping like thunder on the track and beaten the lot of them. He'd claimed the track and won it. It had been the best run of his life.

Dan straightened his hat. 'Come on,' he said. 'We're going out to dinner. The whole hog. We've got a Cup winner to celebrate. And a flaming wedding!'

Aunty Mug looked innocent. 'Wedding?'

'Maureen! You promised!'

Aunty Mug scratched Fred's stomach. 'I did, didn't I? Remember when you promised to take me to the end-of-school dance and went off with Sally Bowker? Remember when you borrowed the ponies from old man Rogers and took me out with them and you swore he'd given you permission and old man Rogers called the police and I lost my pocket money for a month when Dad found out? Remember when you promised I could train Flash Nick and you backed out at the last moment and I gave you your ring back?

Remember when you promised that boat you made was perfectly safe, and . . .'

'Maureen! Those things happened years ago! Now did you or did you not promise that you'd marry me if I helped you with this crazy scheme?'

Aunty Mug smiled. 'I promised I'd marry you Dan Coates. I didn't say when. Ask me in another ten years and see what I say then.'

Annabelle giggled.

'I should have known,' said Dan.

Aunty Mug grinned. She took his arm. 'Come on, grumps. You've survived this long without getting married. You'll survive another ten years or so. Come on, kids. We've got a winner to celebrate.'

'What about Fred?' asked Bernie.

'He's coming too. We're going to the Botanic Gardens. And this old goanna here is going out to buy us the biggest picnic Melbourne's ever seen. With a bottle of sparkling burgundy for me and ginger beer for you two and the best apples in the shop for Fred. Aren't you, Dan?'

'You win,' said Dan.

'I always do,' said Aunty Mug. 'Sometimes it just takes me longer. Now if you'd had me training Irish Lad, Dan Coates, you'd have done a damn sight better than third today.'

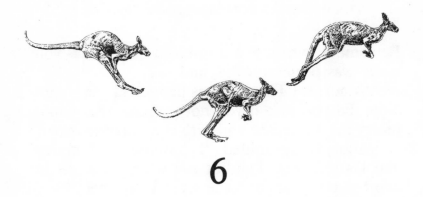

6

The Cup was Fred's last race. He grew restless after Christmas. There were days at a time when he disappeared. The grass shrivelled in the heat and the gum leaves hung limply. A mob of roos moved down from the hills to the fresh grass by the creeks. Fred joined them. He was bigger now than the largest wild buck. His chin was square and his coat had coarsened. For a while, if you saw him in the paddocks, he'd come when he was called, bounding up to the car or horses and reaching for his piece of bread. Finally one day, he ignored them.

Aunty Mug took it philosophically. 'He gave me the most exciting day of my life,' she said. 'If he owes me anything, he's more than repaid it.'

In early January, a parcel came. Annabelle and Bernie found it in the kerosene tin mailbox as they opened the gate to the farm on Saturday morning. The cicadas called above them, and the heat made shimmering waves along the track as they examined the label.

'The kangaroo that won the Cup, Redgate, via Bradley's Bluff,' read Annabelle. They carried it up the track to the house.

The kitchen smelt of wombat droppings and spilt milk. Aunty Mug was feeding Harold. He was out of his sack now, nosing round the kitchen, trying to tunnel through the bread bin and tasting the tea-towels. Pig Iron Bob sharpened his beak on the windowsill beside his cage. The wireless muttered from the mantelpiece: '. . . *those were the first results of race four and it's a fine day here at Flemington with the track in excellent condition . . .*'

'Hey Aunty Mug!' called Annabelle. 'It's a parcel for Fred.'

Aunty Mug put her glasses on and read the label. Then she took them off and looked out the window at the hills.

'Who should open it?' asked Bernie.

'Fred, of course,' said Annabelle. 'It's addressed to him.'

Aunty Mug looked back at them and smiled. 'If Fred ever comes back, we'll show it to him. I don't suppose he'll care. He's got the hills now, and the bush. They mean more to him than any parcel.'

Bernie cut the string. Annabelle unwrapped the paper. There was a cup inside. It gleamed silver against the brown paper. Aunty Mug picked it up and touched it gently.

'Is it the Melbourne Cup?' whispered Annabelle.

Aunty Mug shook her head. 'Not the Melbourne Cup. Take a closer look,' she said, handing it to Annabelle.

It was heavy, and deeply engraved. On one side was a kangaroo leading a field of horses. On the other was written, simply: 'To the Roo that Won the Melbourne Cup.'

'Aunty Mug! You're crying!' exclaimed Bernie.

Aunty Mug reached out and touched the cup again. 'Just a bit of dust in my eye,' she explained. 'Oh darn it. Yes, I'm crying. It's this cup.'

'But it's not the Melbourne Cup,' said Annabelle. 'That's what you said you wanted.'

'Blast the Melbourne Cup,' said Aunty Mug. 'There's dozens of people have got that. But no-one else in the world has won a cup like this. I reckon they never will.'

Bernie put his arms around her. 'You're the only trainer who could ever have done it,' he said. 'There's no-one like you, Aunty Mug.'

'We did it together,' said Aunty Mug. 'You and Annabelle and me and Dan and Fred.'

Bernie paused. 'We had a talk with Dad this morning.'

'We wanted to tell him that we'd thought over all his arguments, but Bernie still wanted to be a farmer and I still wanted to go to vet college,' said Annabelle.

'What did he say?' asked Aunty Mug.

'He just grinned,' said Annabelle. 'I haven't seen him grin like that since Mum died. He said if we could win the Melbourne Cup with a kangaroo, he reckoned we were capable of doing anything we liked.'

'He said the business was doing well enough to employ a mechanic if I didn't want the job. He said Annabelle was just as bad as you, so there was no point in trying to change her.'

'He was laughing,' said Annabelle.

'Then he went back to fixing the super-charger on the Bennetts' Morris Minor,' said Bernie.

Aunty Mug put her arm around their shoulders. 'Told you so,' she said.

No-one has seen Fred for thirty years now. His many times great-grandchildren graze the hills of Redgate. The bush is growing back on the

slopes where the horses once grazed freely.
Today the bark crackles like cornflakes under
their feet as they nose the grass beneath the
trees. There are lots of paddocks for horses,
Aunty Mug reckons, but less and less land in the
world for kangaroos.

Bernie farms the paddocks closer to the
house. His fruit trees shine in the sun and the
scent of ripe peaches is thick enough to float on.
The kitchen is still full of injured animals.
Annabelle takes them out to Aunty Mug when
someone brings them to her veterinary practice
in town, just down the road from Halloran's
Autoworks and Showroom, the best deal on
Holdens around.

Aunty Mug still rides the hills. She's been
doing it for eighty years and says she's not going
to stop now. She still gallops bareback, but not
as often, and not if Dan Coates can see her. Dan
worries. Sometimes when she gallops past a mob
of roos, she hopes that one will prick his ears
and snicker 'Aaaagh' and gallop after her. It
never happens. For, as she says to Dan, there
was only one kangaroo that could ever win the
Melbourne Cup.